T0065589

Separated At Birth

DIANNA LERSSEN

authorHOUSE®

AuthorHouse™
1663 Liberty Drive
Bloomington, IN 47403
www.authorhouse.com
Phone: 1 (800) 839-8640

Published by AuthorHouse 09/14/2016

ISBN: 978-1-5246-3968-6 (sc)
ISBN: 978-1-5246-3967-9 (e)

Print information available on the last page.

This book is printed on acid-free paper.

CHAPTER 1

This is a story about twin girls. They were born to a rich father and a poor mother. Their father Bradley Baker the third fell in love with his best friend, James' girlfriend. Their mother Morgan also fell in love with her boyfriend's friend. The three of them would go to the movies or out dancing. It was always the three of them.

One night when they had gone out dancing Morgan's boyfriend got ill and went home. Morgan tried to go with him but he said, "No, you stay and enjoy yourself. I'm sure Bradley will take you home later. I will call you later, promise." So they stayed and danced for a few hours. It was about 10 p.m. and Morgan said that she needed to get home for school. Bradley said, "Okay" and drove her home.

Morgan asked her mom if James had called her. Mom said, "No, I thought you were out with him and Bradley?" "I was but James wasn't feeling well and told me to stay with Bradley and that he would call me later." She told her mom that she was worried about James and asked if after school if she could walk over there to see if he was better. Mom said she could. Morgan went to bed.

The next day after school she went to James' apartment to see him. She knocked on his door for fifteen minutes and got no answer. She tried the door and it was unlocked. So she walked inside. What she found was James in the living room with the same clothes on from last night. He was setting on the couch with a gun shot to his head. Morgan screamed so loud that the nosy neighbor Miss Lane came right in to see what was going on. Miss Lane grabbed Morgan and dragged her out of there and closed the door.

Miss Lane called the police and told them what she had seen and heard. The spoke to Morgan and asked what she had seen. Morgan just cried. She couldn't speak. Miss Lane being nosy and all told them that Bradley Baker the third was always there and that maybe he knew what happened. So, the police called him and he was therein like five minutes. He stopped and saw Morgan crying very hard and asked the police, "What had happened? Was Morgan okay? Where was James?" That was when Morgan screamed again and yelled, "He's dead!" Then Morgan passed out. The police had Morgan taken home and explained to her mom what had happened. Morgan's mom felt sorry for her. Mom made her some soup and put her to bed.

All night Morgan kept screaming, "I'm sorry" and crying. In the morning her mom asked her what she was sorry for? Morgan looked confused at her mom and asked why she wanted to know? Mom said, "Because that was all you kept saying last night while you were asleep. "Oh, mom" and she started to cry again.

This is why Morgan was so upset and crying. That night when James left early to go home she and Bradley took things too far. Morgan had lost her virginity to Bradley. Morgan and Bradley didn't mean for it to happen but, it did. She wanted to tell James that she was sorry and that it wasn't going to happen again. But found him dead instead. She felt it was her fault that he was dead.

When the police came by to talk to her that Friday they told her that someone had shot and robbed James around 8 p.m. that night. They wanted to know where she and Bradley were at at that time. Morgan told them that they were at the local dance club over on Eighth Street. That Bradley had dropped her home after 10 p.m. due to she had school the next morning. "I'm a senior and I have finals to do." They wrote everything down and said that they would check out her story and get back to her. "Mom, you know me! I loved him. James had asked me the week before to marry him and I had said I would." Morgan started crying again. "Mom in three weeks when school is out I'm going to move and go to college. I love you mom but, I need to get away from this town." That night she called and told Bradley what she was going to do. He said that he wanted to help her if she needed it. Morgan said, "Thank you, your a good friend."

They had services for James that Saturday. Morgan couldn't believe that James was gone and never coming back. She sat there and cried.

Morgan had the ring that James gave her and she handed it to his mom and dad. They looked at her and asked, "When did he do this?" "James had asked me about two weeks ago and we were going to get married this summer. I just felt that I should give this back." They hugged Morgan and told her to keep it, that it was her's. Morgan said, "Thank you" and went home to finish packing.

Morgan had a week left of school and was ready to move on with her life. She just didn't know how.

CHAPTER 2

It had been three months and Morgan didn't go to college like she had planned. Instead she was working at a coffee house. Morgan needed money and lots of it so she could pay the doctor's bills that she was getting. Morgan had found out last month that she was pregnant. Something she didn't plan. She thought of calling Bradley but didn't want to tell him over the phone. She didn't really know how to tell him about the baby. But he did have the right to know.

After work she called Bradley up and asked if he would come up for the weekend so they could talk. Well this made Bradley happy. He hadn't seen Morgan in months. He got there a little after 6 p.m. that Friday night. What he found was a very sad looking Morgan. She asked him to sit down and told him about the job and how she was lucky that they had hired her in her condition. Bradley just looked at her with a puzzled look on his face. Morgan took a deep breath and said, "I'm pregnant with your baby." Morgan braced herself for Bradley to deny the baby.

A few minutes later Bradley jumped up and asked, "When did you find out?" She told him it was last month. Morgan showed him the papers and the little picture. "You really can't see anything yet but in two months they will tell me if it's a girl or a boy." Bradley said that he wanted to be therefor it. He asked if she had told anyone? Morgan looked down and said, "No".

As Bradley was looking around he noticed that her apartment was very tiny and she had only the warn out couch that they sat on in the apartment. Then he saw the stack of bills on the arm. Bradley asked, "What are those? Bills? For what?" Morgan looked up and said, "Those are mostly doctor bills."

"Bradley, I don't want anything from you. I just felt you should know that you are going to be a father." Bradley took Morgan's hands and said, "I don't want our baby in this," as he moved his hand around the apartment. "I will pay for a better place for you and our baby. In fact come back with me and I will do what is right and marry you. I still love you and I can't stop thinking about you. This is a sign. Please marry me, Morgan." Morgan looked up and said, "She was happy with her job and that she didn't want to go back to that town. What would they say? I am with child that was conceived the night James was killed! No, I will stay right here in this town away from my past! You may go home if you wish."

Bradley was heart broken. "I will stay the weekend as planned. Will you at least let me take you out for dinner?" "That will be fine," and Morgan smiled up at Bradley.

While Morgan was in the bathroom getting cleaned up Bradley took her stack of bills and placed them in his pocket. He was going to help her weather she liked it or not. He also took note that she needed some furniture in the apartment. He would have some sent over while he was in town. Bradley walked around the little apartment and noted that there was no bedroom. Bradley didn't like that Morgan was sleeping on that nasty couch. He was going to have to convince Morgan to move to a bigger apartment with a bedroom.

At dinner Bradley told Morgan that he will pay for a bigger apartment because she needed to have a bedroom and a bed to sleep on. "The couch isn't good for the baby or you. Please, let me help you out". "I don't want to take anything from you. This is my fault. I let things go too far that night. Now I pay for it the rest of my life." Bradley took her hands and said, "We both did this and we both will pay. I want to start now." Morgan gave in and said, "Okay, but we tell no one about this. Our families will not know till the baby is born." "Deal!" Bradley smiled and was very pleased with how things were going.

That night he convinced Morgan to stay at the hotel with him. The next morning Bradley and Morgan went looking for a bigger apartment. "Ah, here's a nice one and it has two bedrooms, so the baby will have a room too." But it cost three times what I pay now." "Yes, but you live in a shack of an apartment too. This is the one you are getting and that's that!"

Morgan said, "Okay" and she signed the lease along with Bradley. Bradley said that he had to sign it due to him paying the rent.

Two months later Bradley came down for the doctor's visit to see if he would get a son or a daughter. He was excited and could hardly wait for Morgan to get off work so they could go. When he seen Morgan step around the counter he was shocked to see how big she had gotten. Morgan looked so tired. He felt sad that she wouldn't let him pay 100% of everything. But, he loved that about her. Bradley was going to ask her again to marry him. He was going to ask after they found out what she was having.

An hour later they were in the waiting room to be seen. Morgan was so tired that she was leaning over on his shoulder asleep. He just sat there with the biggest smile he had had in months. He loved Morgan and he knew she loved him but he couldn't understand why she kept saying no to him. Hopefully today she would say yes. Finally after setting there for another hour they got called back. At first they tried to stop him from going back with her but Morgan said that he was the father. That she wanted him in there with her. She wanted him with her. Bradley was getting his hopes up.

The doctor came in and asked, "How are you feeling? Are you still having cramps?" Cramps? He didn't know she was having any problems. The doctor looked at Bradley and said, "Hello" and asked if they were ready to see what they were having? Bradley was the first to answer with a yes. Morgan said that she was ready to see her baby too. So, the doctor got the machine ready and had Morgan pull her shirt up so he could put the gel on. As she did this Bradley saw her belly move. Bradley asked the doctor if that was the baby? The doctor laughed a little and said, "Yes."

"Okay little mamma you ready?" Morgan just smiled. Bradley reached for her hand and held on to it. "Okay here we go then." The doctor moved the machine over Morgan's belly and there was our baby. The doctor kept moving around and said, "Ah." Bradley asked if everything was okay with the baby and Morgan? The doctor turned to look at both of them and said, "The babies are fine. It's girls." Morgan and I just stared at each other and then the doctor. "Babies? What do you mean babies? I thought I was having a baby?" Morgan asked. "Well the first picture we did when you first came in didn't show a second baby due to she must have been hiding behind her sister. From the way it looks they will be identical twin girls.

Which means they are in the same sac. When you conceived your egg split and formed two babies," explained the doctor. Then Morgan started to cry.

As they were getting into Bradley's car Morgan looked up at him and said, "I can't raise two babies alone." Bradley said, "You don't have to, marry me." Morgan replied, "I can't, not right now. I'm sorry Bradley, I love you, but not now." Bradley looked at her sadly and asked what she wanted to do with the girls. "That's simple, you take one and I will take one." "You want to separate the girls!? Why?" "Just till I can think everything out. Our families are not going to be happy with us. Your family won't be happy that you had a baby with a poor girl." "Screw my family! Morgan you and the girls are my family now." Morgan just sat there and cried.

Bradley came down every weekend to make sure she had everything that she needed. They got the baby room ready. Bradley had the room painted a soft purple with red roses. Then they sat there and talked about what to name the girls. Morgan said she wanted the girls to have the same name just is a different order. That way we will always remember the other girl. Bradley agreed to it and they went to bed.

At eight months Morgan went into labor and had a nurse call Bradley. He was still at his home three towns away. Morgan hoped that he would get there in time. About an hour later as the doctor was telling Morgan to start pushing Bradley ran in. "Did I miss it?" The doctor said, "No, you got here just in time." Bradley washed his hands and went to Morgan.

Morgan pushed for two hours before the two girls were born. They were perfect. Bradley bent over and kissed Morgan without thinking and she kissed him back. The doctor asked what were their names? Morgan said, "Mary Rose Baker and Rose Mary Baker. After their father." Morgan went to sleep and left Bradley to tend to the girls. Bradley was a very proud father. He had a nurse take a picture of him holding both of the girls. He wanted to remember this day forever. He was going to have a copy made for Morgan so she would remember him being there with her.

A week later Morgan and the girls were released from the hospital. Bradley drove them home. Morgan had a month off work so she had lots of time to fall in love with both of the girls. During that month Bradley stayed with Morgan and the girls. He loved Morgan even more that he did last year. But, she won't marry him. At least not right now, she had said. Maybe when the girls were bigger. Bradley looked into all the day cares in the area. He wanted the best care his little girl could have and he didn't care what the cost was.

The day came when Morgan had to go back to work and he had to go back home with Mary. He still wasn't sure how he was going to tell his dad or grandfather about Mary. Bradley drove Rose to the daycare that he had picked and talked to the lady there. He gave her his number and address if they needed him to be there for Rose. He kissed Rose good-bye and walked out the door with Mary in his arms. He then went to the coffee house and dropped off a set of car keys for Morgan and the picture he had taken at the hospital the day the girls were born and one of the four of them with a note. Bradley then walked out and drove home to speak to his family about Mary Rose.

CHAPTER 3

I t had been four years today the last time he saw Morgan and Rose Mary. He was there for her first birthday. The girls looked just like each other. I love Morgan and Rose Mary so much and missed them too. Today was the girls fifth birthday. He had lost touch with Morgan after the girls had their first birthday. They had just disappeared. Morgan had quit her job and taken Rose out of the day care and left her apartment. Today the girls are five. Mary is so smart and she is always happy. She looks so much like Morgan it wasn't funny. Mary had Morgan's blue eyes and blonde wavy hair. Bradley wondered if Rose had his eyes but then again the girls are mirror image. So he guessed not. The only thing the girls had that was of him was his tan skin and nose. Everything else was Morgan.

As Bradley was driving home from the toy store he thought he saw Morgan walking. He thought that was odd because she said that she would never come back to this town. As he turned the corner he looked back and didn't see her. Wow, his mind was playing tricks with him today. That's what he gets for thinking about Morgan and Rose Mary. I wonder if she has married or has anymore kids? I haven't been able to think about being with anyone else. I just want Morgan and Rose to be home with me and Mary. The girls need to be together.

When he got home for the party, Mary ran out to the car yelling, «Daddy, daddy!! Grandpa got me a horsey!» Then she pulled out a picture and said very quietly, «I was a bad girl. I went in your room and found a pick-ture. Who is the lady with the two babies and you daddy?» Bradley took the photo and looked down at it. It was the picture he had taken at the girls first birthday. The last time he saw Rose and Morgan. Bradley looked down at his little girl and said, «Iᵭll tell you later, sweetheart. Now, show me this horsey.» «Oᵭtay daddy,» and Mary ran off into the house. Boy, I hope my dad didnᵭt see this picture. I know my dad would realize who the girl is and that Mary had a twin sister.

Bradley dismissed the thought and went inside. He didn't think Mary showed anyone the picture. Mary was a very smart little girl. Whenever she did something wrong she always came and told him first. No matter how long she had to wait to tell him. He loved her so much. His little princess. He smiled and knocked on his father's study door. He wanted to speak to him before he seen Mary's new horsey.

When his father told him he could enter Bradley stepped inside. As Bradley was shutting the door he was shocked to see Morgan in the study talking to his father. Bradley didn't know what to say. He just stared at Morgan. Mr. Baker cleared his throat and told his son to sit down. Bradley did as he was told. Still he couldn't take his eyes off of Morgan. She was standing there in front of his father with her head down and her hands in front of her. God, she looked great. Just like he remembered her.

"Well, if you are done gawking at the new help please let me know." Help? "Umm, yes father, sorry." "Well this young lady is in need of a job and I thought that I should hire her. She has an ad in the local paper that she could be a live in nanny as long as she could bring her young daughter as well. I thought that would be great for Mary. She looks so lonely when you are gone at work. So, I was telling Miss Worn that she could have the job and that she would be paid 12.00 dollars an hour minus the time that Mary is asleep or out with you. Her little girl is named Rose and is out back with Mary, so I am told. I have not seen the little girl yet. Miss Worn was telling me that today was Rose's birthday and that she is five. Isn't that great!?" Bradley couldn't speak. Hell, he couldn't breathe right now. He had to get out of there and fast. Bradley stood and explained that he needed to go check on Mary and make sure that her gifts were put up. Then he turned and almost ran into the door.

Outside his father's door he leaned against it. I can't believe they are here, in my father's. Outside? Rose was outside with Mary! Bradley ran to the back door and as he was reaching for the door knob the cook Mrs. Golden asked him to come speak to her. Mrs. Golden had been like a mother to him and he always told her everything. But he never told her about the girls. He was in trouble with her now. "Yes Mrs. Golden? May I help you with something?" Bradley asked with a big smile on his face. "You sure can help me young man." Mrs. Golden was standing by the oven with her hands on her hips. "Why you no tell me about Mary's mama? I saw a little girl come thought here and when I called her Mary she stopped and said her name was Rose and that Mary was her middle name. Why on earth is there a little girl running around that looks just like little Mary but isn't Mary?" Mrs. Golden asked while tapping her foot. "Umm".... "Out with it boy! I want the whole story now. I didn't help raise you to hide things from me. I could of helped you out."

Bradley sighed and explained to Mrs. Golden the whole story and that Morgan was speaking to his father now about being Mary's live in nanny. "I don't think Morgan knew that he was my father and it was going to be Mary till she got here. "You mean that poor girl who left town after her boyfriend was killed?" "Yes, ma'am. Father hasn't seen Rose yet. He's going to flip when he see's the two girls together." "Boy, I glad I ani't you right now." I wish I wasn't me right now either. Anyways, I gotta run and get Rose some gifts too. I just wanted to get a peek at Rose and Mary. I haven't seen them together since their first birthday." "Well I can tell you she is just as pretty as Mary." Bradley smiled and walked out the door.

When he got to the play area his father had made for Mary he stood there and just looked around. He didn't see the two girls at first. They were hiding up in the tree house. All Bradley could hear was a bunch of laughter. That sound just made him smile big to himself. He thought to himself, this is the sound I would of heard all these years if Morgan had said yes to him when she told him she was with child or in this case children. Bradley was so caught up in his own thoughts that he didn't hear his father come out and stand by him. What he did hear was Mary yelling for Rose to stop before she fell. Just as Bradley looked up to see what was wrong Rose fell from the tree house and straight into his father's arms.

"I'm sorry sir," was the little voice that came out od Rose. Bradley's father smiled and said, "Call me grandfather or papa Baker." Rose looked up and said very softly that she wasn't allowed because she didn't have a grandfather anymore that he passed away last year. Also that her grandmother passed away last week. "My mamma said that I'm to say yes sir or no sir and yes ma'am or no ma'am." Mr. Baker smiled and said that it was very good that she did what her mamma told her. That he was sure that she wouldn't get into trouble for calling him those names. "I will ask my mamma first please," Rose stated. Mr. Baker sat her down and Rose ran to the house and straight into her mamma's arms.

Well Rose told her mamma everything that had happened and her mamma looked up and mouthed, "Thank you," to Mr. Baker. Morgan than took Rose by the hand to go clean up.

Mr. Baker that turned to his only son and told him to explain everything about Morgan and Rose. Bradley told his father he would inside after he talked to Mary about Rose and Morgan. Mr. Baker said, "Fine, but you only have an hour because he wanted to know before the party started due to the fact that he was going to inform everyone of his other granddaughter that was hidden from him the past five years." As Mr. Baker was walking away Bradley yelled, "Did you ask Morgan if you could do that?" His father replied that Morgan was working for him and that he could do as he pleased in his own home. With that said he went to his study and shut the door.

CHAPTER 4

Bradley took Mary to the toy store after his father went inside so they could get Rose something for her birthday. Mary asked her daddy why they was getting Rose a gift on her birthday. Bradley parked the car and looked at his little princess and told her that Rose was really her twin sister and that Miss Worn was her mamma. "My mamma? I have a mamma and a sister? Oh, daddy, thank you for them! I love my birthday gifts." Mary yelled and wrapped her little arms around her daddy's neck and giving him a kiss on the cheek. Mary was very happy hearing this news even though she really didn't understand what was being told to her.

Mary picked out a pretty baby doll and some clothes for it. She picked out a big teddy bear that was purple with red roses all over it. She explained to daddy that is was the roses that caught her eyes. That roses was for Rose. Bradley looked down at her and smiled and said that it was very nice of her to think that way. As they were putting the toys in the trunk, Mary said she wanted to get Rose a pretty dress like the one she was going to wear that day for the party. Bradley said, "Okay." They walked over to the Lil' Miss dress shop. Bradley told Mary that it should be a different color so everyone would know who was who. Mary giggled and said, "O'tay daddy." Mary's dress was a bright yellow dress with white roses all over it. So they picked out a white dress with bright yellow roses on it. "Rosie going to like this dress daddy," Mary yelled.

At the house Mr. Baker was talking to the cake shop on his phone explaining that he needed a second cake with a different name on it. The cake shop try to say they could not have one done in time but Mr. Baker would not hear of it. "You have three hours to get both cakes here or I will never business with you again!" Mr. Baker hung the phone up after giving them the details for the second cake. Mr. Baker looked around to see how everything was coming together for the party. The back yard looked good to him, then he spotted the birthday sign. It read:

HAPPY BIRTHDAY MARY ROSE! Mr. Baker studied that sign for a good while before it clicked. Mary Rose? Hmmm....

Mr. Baker went into the house and call Miss Worn down to the kitchen. Morgan walked in with little Rose right behind her. "You called me sir?" Morgan asked with head down. "Yes, I have a question about your little girl there," he replied pointing at Rose. "What is her middle name?" Before Morgan could say anything Rose spoke up and said that it was Mary. After she said that she hid behind her mamma before he could look at her really good. She was suppose to stayed up stairs but because no one was up there she had followed so she wouldn't be alone in the big house.

Morgan started to cry, "I'm sorry Mr. Baker." I didn't mean to keep everything a to myself. Please don't be upset with Bradley. I made him keep Rose a secret. I didn't want anyone thinking bad thoughts about him and I didn't think you would approved of me." Mr. Baker stood there very quite while Morgan pleaded with him. "I thought that if you knew Bradley had a child with me that you would take her away from me and I would never see her again. But, when we found out it was twins I thought that it would be better that Bradley take one and I would keep one. I now know that I should not have asked Bradley to keep us a secret. I'm so sorry Mr. Baker. I just didn't want to lose both of them. I thought I'd be okay just losing one of the girls." Mr. Baker still did not speak.

"What would you have me done? Give up both girls? I couldn't do that. I didn't really want to give Mary up but I had made a promise to Bradley that he would take Mary with him. I didn't want him to be without his daughters. So, I felt if we each took one home then no one was losing a daughter. So, I thought at the time. That was the main reason the two girls have the same name just in a different order. It was so we wouldn't forget our other daughter. That a part of her was still with us." Morgan just kept crying with her hands up to her face.

The whole time Rose was listening to her mamma talk about how she was a secret and everything. Rose was confused about what was being said. Rose pulled at her mamma and was trying to ask her why she was feeling so sad and what did all of this mean? "Mamma? Mamma? Talk to me. I don't understand," and then Rose started to cry too. Mr. Baker still didn't speak.

CHAPTER 5

Bradley and Mary was walking in the front door when they heard Rose and Morgan crying. Mary not thinking and after hearing all the news of everything, she runs into the room and yells, "Grandpa! Why you making my mamma ans sissy cry!? That's not nice!" After she yelled all that she covered her mouth and ran behind her daddy.

Well, Bradley was as shocked as his father was at Mary's out burst. Bradley looked down at Mary and told her to take Rose up to her room while the big people talked. Mary said, "O'tay daddy" and went to Rose and pulled on her hand a little and said, "Rosie lets go play in my, I mean our room now. What's mine is yours too." She said all of this with the biggest smile ever. This was the first time the three adults saw the girls side by side. It was like they were looking in a mirror. The only difference was that Mary was wearing a dress and Rose was in a pair of cut off shorts that her mamma made and an old t-shirt. Rose's hair was pulled back into a messy ponytail and Mary's hair was down and messy from playing outside earlier. Mary had forgotten to brush her hair before they went to the store but Bradley didn't care at the time. But instead of the two girls went out back to play.

After the two girls out od sight Bradley said to hid father and to Morgan that he was sorry. He ran his hand thought his hair and looked every where but at his father. Everyone was quite for a few minutes. It was Mr. Baker that spoke first. He turned to Morgan and very calmly asked her she felt that she should of had the girls separated all these years. I would of loved to been allowed to get to know both of my granddaughter's and as well as my father before he passed away.

All poor Morgan could think to say was, "Sorry sir." Bradley walked over to Morgan and tried to put his arm around her but she stepped out of his reach. She looked up at Bradley and said that she didn't know this was his dad's address. That she didn't speak with him that she spoken to a Mrs. Golden. "Rose and I will leave right away." Morgan tried to turn but Bradley looked down at Morgan and said, "No, you can't take her from Mary, not now." Then Mr. Baker said very sternly, "No one is taking my granddaughter anywhere!" The look that Morgan gave him was down right murderous, "You will not stop me from taking my daughter away from here!" Then Morgan started to cry. With her hands in her face she fell into a chair and cried. Bradley walk over to Morgan and helped her up out of the chair and over to the big window. Told her to look out the window at the two girls and say she would rip them apart again.

As Morgan looked out the window in Mr. Baker's kitchen she watched how the two girls played as one, like they had played together everyday their whole life. Not just today. They walked as one. If one moved to the left the other did it without thinking. They were laughing now at something the other had said. Morgan put her head down and said, "They would stay but only for the girls." She knew she couldn't separate the two girls now. In her heart she wanted to stay for Bradley too, but she wasn't going to say that out loud, she was too proud to admit that she missed his as much as she had missed Mary.

Morgan turned away from the window and asked where her room would be so that she may get cleaned up before the party that was being held for Mary. Mr. Baker told her where her room was and said that the party was for both girls. Now that Rose was here she would get the same attention as Mary did from now on. Morgan started to say something but thought it best to keep it to herself. She knew she was on the losing team. With no real job Mr. Baker was sure to take Rose from her if he felt he needed to.

When Morgan got up to her room she looked around. It was done up very nice. The bed was made of cherry wood. The bedspread was a like purple with cherry blossoms coming up from the bottom. She had a small table with a reading lamp on it. Next to that was a soft reading chair done up in a dark purple fabric. She had a cherry wood dressing table and her own bathroom. Which was done up in light blue tiles. Morgan was glad to see that it had a bathtub and a stand alone shower. In her bathroom she saw that her one suitcase was setting on a small stand. She walked over to it and opened it up.

After her shower she felt much better. She thought to herself, I better get the girls cleaned up and dressed. After all I'm getting paid to care for my own daughter. Morgan had already made Mr. Baker upset with her and she didn't want him more upset and throw her out and keep Rose from her. She would be nothing without Rose. She had given up all her old dreams just to care for Rose and she was doing a good job so far or at least she thought she was anyways.

CHAPTER 6

It was getting close to the time for the twins birthday party and to introduce Rose to the rest of the family. Both the girls were up stairs getting their pretty party dresses on. Mary put on her bright yellow dress with little white roses and Rose put on the dress that Mary picked out for her, which was a white dress with bright yellow roses. After they had their dresses on they got their hair done. The hair dresser that Mr. Baker hired put banana curls in their hair and placed matching crowns on top of their heads. The crowns were done up with real diamonds. Rose stood in front of the mirror looking at herself. She couldn't believe that she was dressed up so pretty and had a sister who looked just like her. She was so happy.

Rose had never worn a dress this pretty before. Morgan couldn't afford to get dresses like this one. Rose thought to herself, I hope we stay here forever. I love having a sister and a daddy and also a grandpa again. I at least hope that they like me enough to let us stay.

Two hours later Mary and Rose came down to show off their looks to their parents and grandpa. As they reached the bottom stairs everyone looked up and was so surprised at how much they looked like Morgan. The girls were perfect in every way. The girls asked if they looked o'tay because the adults were all just staring at them.

Looking at the two girls Bradley realized that he missed too much of Rose growing up and was sadden with the fact that she and Morgan had moved out of the apartment that he was paying for and then they had disappeared. He had tried to find her and Rose for the last three years with no luck. Then out of the blue they were in his home. He would make sure they didn't disappear again.

Mr. Baker was the one that said that the girls looked perfect and that the crowns he ordered only an hour ago looked great on them. He now had two granddaughter prenicess's. Mr. Baker cleared his throat and said, "Let's go girls." With a big smile he had them go to the kitchen and stand at the back door.

As the two girls entered the back yard Mr. Baker cleared his throat and announced the two girls to the guest, "We have princess Mary Rose Baker and her twin sister, princess Rose Mary Baker." The two girls waved hi.

Some of the guest gasped at the fact that the girls were identical. The guest looked at each other and whispered about the girls and how they only had gifts for one of the girls. Mr. Baker cleared his throat and everyone got quite. "I understand that you were all expecting one birthday girl and it is alright, her father and I have taken the liberty of getting Rose Mary enough gifts that she has the same amount as Mary Rose." The guest looked relieved.

The party was different from what Rose was used to. The party had a little mini petting zoo and a bunch of balloons. There was a guy doing magic tricks and another one making balloon animals. The had pony rides too. Rose was so excited with everything. As she looked around she saw that there were four tables stacked with gifts and another table had two cakes. All she could do was look at everything. Rose didn't know what to do.

Mary came over to Rose and said, "Come on Rosie the ponies are for us to ride." Mary dragged Rose by her hand to the pony rides. There were a few kids running around the party. As Rose was dragged, Mary would point and tell her who the kid was as they passed them. "That's cousin Maggie and That's cousin Ricky over there, by the cakes is cousin Johnny, Eddie, and David. They are brothers and they can be mean so watch out for them. Over by the gifts is uncle Frank and his wife aunt Beth and their daughter Jessie. Jessie is cool, she is fifteen and loves to do my hair. So, you will love her." There were so many adults and some other kids that Rose couldn't keep up with who was who. All she knew was they were family and friends of daddy and grandpa.

"Wow!" Rose thought. "I got's a big family now. I hope they all like me as much as Mary likes me. Grandpa must like me too because he and daddy got me lots of gifts to open. I didn't know where I will put all my new things."

The girls had fun at their birthday party. They mostly rode the ponies until their grandpa said it was time for the gifts and cake. The guest all stood around the cake table and sang, "HAPPY BIRTHDAY" to the two girls. The girls blew out their candles on their cakes and told everyone, "THANK YOU." The cakes were marble with pink and purple icing. Mary had a cake with Barbie on it and Rose had a cake with Tinker Bell on it. The girls loved their cakes.

While the girls opened their gifts the guest ate cake. Rose was only half way through the gifts and she was getting tired. So far Rose and Mary had gotten twenty new dresses and matching shoes. Rose got a bright purple bed set with butterflies in dark purple on it. Rose also got a big brown teddy bear the size of her mamma and a big purple teddy bear with red roses all over it and a baby doll with a bunch of clothes from Mary and daddy. Rose and Mary each got a big red bouncy ball. Rose got a jewelry box filled with everything from grandpa. Mary had gotten a new necklace with her name on it from grandpa. Plus they had other toys and clothes. Mrs. Golden even got Rose and Mary matching baby dolls that were really soft to the touch. Rose was in the middle of opening her next gift when she fell asleep. Morgan went to get her when Bradley got to her first. Rose snuggled closer to him and stayed asleep. Mary saw this and asked Morgan to carry her to their room too. Morgan smiled and picked Mary up. Mary gave Morgan a big hug and said, "I love you mamma and thank you for coming back home for me." Mary then closed her eyes. Morgan just kept smiling.

When they got to the girls room, Morgan asked Bradley to take Rose to her room until the got a bed for Rose in Mary's room. Bradley just smiled and opened Mary's door and told Morgan to go inside. When Morgan stepped inside Mary's room was different. There were now two matching canopy beds with the girls names hanging on the wall just above the headboards. The canopy beds were cherry wood with little roses and angels carved into the posts. The canopy tops were a soft blue as well as the beding. They laid the girls in the beds with their names. Gave them kisses on the foreheads and closed the door behind them. Morgan looked up at Bradley and just smiled at him.

Morgan couldn't believe that she was here with Bradley. She never thought that she would see him again after she had moved out of the apartment he was paying for. But here he was all 6′3″ of him. His hair was still dark brown and he still had his cute goatee that she had loved. He was still thin but manly thin. His eyes looked like they were maybe a bit darker than she remember them being. She thought that they were a soft gray but today they looked to be a dark gray. Oh well, she didn't care she still loved him but didn't want to tell him. She would let him make the first move. That is if he didn't have a girlfriend.

Later that night at dinner, the two girls were talking to each other about their gifts. Rose was saying that she had never gotten so many gifts before and couldn't believe that grandpa and daddy had time to get her anything. She only ever got two things a year. One thing from mamma and one thing from her grandma and grandpa on mamma's side. With that Rose looked over at mamma and asked what she had gotten her this year? With a sad smile Morgan said that she couldn't get her anything this year. That was when Bradley took Morgan's hands and placed two small boxes into her hands. He looked into her eyes and said, "These are from you to the girls."

So, Morgan handed the little boxes to the girls and inside was a locket for them to wear. Inside the locket was a baby picture of the two girls on one side and a picture of Morgan and Bradley. On the outside of the locket, on the front was their names and on the back it said, "With much love, mommy and daddy." The girls looked up at their parents and smiled really big. At the same time the girls said, "We love it!"

CHAPTER 7

Morgan and Rose have been at the Bake's home for a month now. The two girls did everything together as though they were never apart all those years. Morgan found herself always with a smile on her face. Morgan loved being with both girls. She even found herself smiling when Bradley came home after work and played with the girls. Morgan was falling deeper in love with Bradley but didn't know if he felt the same way about her after all these years.

One morning Mary came to Morgan and asked, "Are you and Rosie going to stay here forever?" Morgan didn't know what to say. She looked down at her daughter and told her, "For now they would stay but they needed to find their own home to live in." This didn't make Mary happy at all. Mary ran to her daddy crying that mamma was going to leave and take Rosie away. Mary looked up at her daddy and said, "Please, make mamma and Rosie stay. I don't want to lose my mamma and sissy." Bradley looked at his daughter in his arms and gave her a big hug and tried to reassure her that they weren't going anywhere.

After Bradley sent Mary up to her room to play with Rose he went to find and speak with Morgan. He didn't like it when his little princess was upset. He wanted to tell Morgan that she had to stay for the girls. Also, he wanted Morgan to marry him and only him.

Bradley found Morgan in the library looking at a photo album. When he got closer to where she was setting he saw that she was crying. Morgan had found Mary's baby book. Bradley put his hand on Morgan's shoulder and asked her why she was upset. Morgan looked up into Bradley's electric blue eyes and all she could say was, "Sorry." She looked back down at the book. This wasn't what he expected to find when he went looking for Morgan. Bradley sat down next to Morgan on the leather couch. He then took the book off of Morgan's lap and made her look up at him. All his earlier rage gone.

"Look, Morgan, we have a chance to start fresh and be a family with the girls." Bradley told her. Morgan said, "How? I'm still a poor girl and I'm now working for your father of all people." She sigh, "I'm getting paid to watch my own daughter!" Morgan got up and ran out of the room crying. Bradley didn't know how to make Morgan see that she belonged here poor or not.

When Morgan had ran out of the room she ran straight into Mr. Baker. He was looking for her because he wanted to speak to her about the two girls. He didn't sound happy either. Just what she needed Mr. Baker upset with her yet again. Having Mr. Baker upset with her was not a good ideal. Morgan tried to go around him but he would not have it. Mr. Baker looked at her and said very sternly, "Miss Worn, I'd like to speak with you in my study, now!" So, with her head down Morgan walked with Mr. Baker to his study and shut the door behind her. She braced herself for whatever he was going to throw at her this time.

CHAPTER 8

Later that night Bradley heard Morgan speaking to his father in his study and she didn't sound happy nor did his father. "You want to speak with me, sir?" Asked Morgan. "Yes, it seems that my granddaughter Mary is always in tears since you have been here. Why is that, Miss Worn? This last time I hear you are wanting to leave and take my other granddaughter away. Am I not giving you enough money? Do you want more? Well, answer me when I speak to you!" Mr. Baker yelled. "I need a paying job so I can support my girls," he heard Morgan said. Then his father spoke in a gruff tone, "You are being paid to take care of my granddaughter! How dare you say that you need a job that pays!" "You don't understand, Brad! You never did!" Yelled Morgan. "I knew that I shouldn't have came back to this town! Besides, I shouldn't be paid to be with my daughter, Mary! If I had a place to go I'd take my girls and leave! This is why I always said no to Bradley when he asked me to marry him." "You are not going to take my granddaughters ever!" Yelled Mr. Baker.

Bradley was confused. What was his father and Morgan talking about? When did they talk before?

He was about to walk in when Morgan ran from the room and almost ran right into Bradley. Bradley reached out to stop her but she side stepped him and ran out the front door and got into her car.

When the car started he saw Rose run out the door yelling for her mamma. Then he saw Mary follow as well and both girls got into the backseat and Morgan drove off. This made Bradley panic. Where was she going with both of the girls? He hoped they would be back soon because it was close to dinner time. He didn't like that his daughter went anywhere without him. He knew that Morgan was her mother but he had no clue where they went or when they would be back.

Morgan didn't plan on the two girls jumping into the car when she was trying to leave. She didn't have the heart to tell them to get out and go back into the house. Although, it was nice being out with the two girls alone. While out she drove by a few shops and found one that had clothes that would fit her. So she stopped and parked the car in front of Lowman's Clothing For Young Women. The two girls helped her get some new clothes. She got three pairs of jeans and five t-shirts. A pair of sandals. Also, in the back of the store she was able to get some new bra's and panties. She liked this store and would need to remember to come here again if she needed anymore clothes.

After they shopped for clothes for herself, they went to the Pizza Place for dinner. The girls ate cheese pizza and she had a salad. This place was better than she remembered. Mary and Rose enjoyed their outing with their mamma. When they were done with their pizza, Morgan asked the girls if they wanted to go anywhere. Mary said that she would like to go to the big toy store. Morgan looked into her wallet to see if she had enough money in case the girls found something they wanted. Morgan had thirty dollars left and told the girls, "Okay, let's go."

At the toy store where Mary had been lots of times with her daddy and grandpa. Mary said to her mamma, "Tis way to babies mamma." Mary grabbed Morgan and Rose's hands and pulled them down to the baby dolls. Rose had never been in a toy store with so many toys. She was amazed with all the different types of toys. So, Rose kept stopping and looking at everything.

As they went down one of the aisles they passed a lady who knew Mary and stopped them before they got to the dolls. "Mary, where is your daddy and who is this little girl and lady....?" The woman was caught by surprise when she took a good look at the other little girl and lady. "Morgan Worn is that you?" The woman asked. Morgan said, "Yes, Who are y...? Oh, No!" It was James mother, Mrs. Heartman. Morgan was looking around and trying to hide the girls behind her when Rose said, "Mamma, I can't see the lady." Mrs. Heartman looked at Morgan and mouthed, mamma? "When did you had a child and why does she look like Mary, Bradley Baker's daughter?' Then Mrs. Heartman looked closer at the two girls then back at Morgan. "Oh, so this is why you left town five years ago? You were cheating on my son with his best friend! How could you? He loved you!" With that Mrs. Heartman walked out of the store. Great now the whole town is going to know that I had twins with Bradley. Mary looked up at her mamma and said, "It's o'tay mamma, daddy don't like her either. Daddy calls her a big mouth. I don't know why? She has a little mouth like you." Morgan smiled down at her daughter and said, "Okay, where are these babies you wanted to show me?"

It was well pass dinner time and bedtime for the girls when Morgan pulled into the driveway. Bradley ran outside and hugged Morgan as she got out of the car. "I was so worried about you and the girls!" Bradley exclaimed. "Did you and the girls eat?" Bradley asked as he held her at arms length. With a yawn Morgan just nodded her head to say yes. Bradley opened the back door to get one of the sleeping girls out. He had gotten Rose out and she opened her sleep filled eyes at him. She smiled and then closed her eyes again with a sigh and said, "Wub you daddy." Bradley smiled and headed for the house with her. Morgan got Mary out on the other side and shut the door. Mary yawned and said, "Wub you mamma," and closed her eyes and hugged Morgan tight. Morgan smiled and walked into the house.

Once they had the girls in their nightgowns and tucked into bed for the night, Bradley took Morgan by the arm and lead her to her room across the hall. Bradley opened her door and lead her inside and shut the door behind him. "For the love of God, Morgan, please don't scare me like that again!" Bradley exclaimed. Morgan raised her hand up to silent him. "I did nothing wrong for you to worry. I went out and the girls wanted to come with me. They are both mine as well as yours." Morgan said calmly. "Both yours! I think not, you haven't been here to help raise Mary. I was, my father and grandfather were!" Bradley exclaimed. Bradley took a deep breath and in a low voice said, "You didn't want us." With sad eyes Bradley left the room.

The next morning Bradley and Morgan avoided each other. If one of them was with the girls the other one would go somewhere else in the house. Neither one of them said a word to the other most of the day. Finally at dinner time when everyone was at the dinner table the spoke. Morgan said, "I'm sorry for leaving with both girls without a word to you,

Bradley." Morgan explained that she was upset and wasn't planning on the girls coming with her but was glad they did for they had cheered her up. Especially after she had ran into James' mother, Mrs. Heartman and she had yelled at her in front of the girls. Bradley said that it was fine and that he was sorry for over reacting when she had gotten back. That he was also sorry that she ran into Mrs. Heartman while out with the girls. That was all they said to each other at the dinner table. Mr. Baker said that he would speak to Mrs. Heartman in the morning. He was displeased that the women had the nerve to yell in front of the girls. He would not have this kind of behavior around his granddaughters.

After they put the girls to bed Bradley tried to speak to Morgan about the outing yesterday. Morgan raised her hand to stop him and said that with what had gone on yesterday and today that she had forgotten to get the girls new babies out of the car and her new clothes out of the trunk. Bradley said that he would go get them and then turned to Morgan and asked how she had gotten the dolls, food and herself some clothes? Morgan looked up at him and said that his father was still paying her to look after Mary and went into her room. Bradley was knocking on her bedroom door ten minutes later with her bags. Morgan said to come in and he did. Bradley asked if she needed help putting her things away? Without thinking of what she had bought and what was in the bags she told him that he could help.

The first bag that Bradley started to put away he ended up with a hand full of panties. With a big smile on his face he asked Morgan, "Where do you want me to put your umm panties?" With a red face Morgan said that she had forgot that she had gotten those and took them from Bradley and placed them into the top drawer of the dressing table. Then she took that bag from him and placed it under the chair. The rest of the clothes got hung in the closet. Morgan told Bradley, "Thank you for the help." Bradley smiled and said, "Anytime if I find more of your panties to put away." Then he left her room to go to his room for the night.

CHAPTER 9

Morgan and Rose have been living with the Baker's now for three months. Mary and Rose did everything together. Mr. Baker had placed both of the girls in a private school and had made sure they were in the same class. He didn't want the girls apart for now.

Everyday when the girls came in from school they would run to Morgan yelling, "Mamma! Mamma! Guess what we did today?" They would tell her what story the teacher, Miss Nikki read to them. They would tell her what they colored and always had a picture for her and daddy to put on the fridge. They would tell her if anyone got into trouble and what Miss Nikki made then do. They would tell her what game they learned to play and they always wanted her and daddy to play the new games when daddy got home from work. Morgan always loved hearing about their day at school. It always made her smile. When they were done telling her everything she would send the girls off to tell their grandpa. Which they did happily everyday.

While the girls told grandpa about their day Morgan would find a spot on the living room wall to hang the newest pictures. The wall by now was very colorful with all the different pictures up. There were pictures that they drew and ones that they tried to color. Her favorite one was the ones the girls did of the family. There was her and Bradley with the girls and ones with everyone in the house. They even added their horses. Mr. Baker was the funny pictures that were up. The girls had drawn him with a long beard and he had gifts all around him. The pictures said Grandpa Santa. Of course Mr. Baker didn't have a beard but it did seem he always had something new for the girls every week.

That night at dinner the girls repeated their day to their daddy. He would listen with a smile on his face. He loved both the girls very much and wanted the best for them. Tonight for dinner they were having pot roast with carrots, potatoes and celery. This was the girls favorite dish that Mrs. Golden made. For desert they had banana splits with extra whip cream on top. While at dinner Mr. Baker told Morgan that she had tomorrow off and that he would be taking both the girls out for the day. Morgan started to say something but the look she got from Mr. Baker made her close her mouth. So Morgan just nodded her head. She then asked to be excused from the table and went to her room.

Later that night Bradley went to Morgan's room and knocked. Morgan said, "Come in." Bradley walked in and saw that Morgan was reading a book and cleared his throat. When Morgan looked up, it looked like she had been crying. Bradley walked over to her and asked if she was alright. Bradley placed his hand on her shoulder and Morgan leaned into him. "I don't know what to do? I should be paying your father for staying here. I mean I shouldn't be paid to watch my own daughter." Bradley pulled her up from the chair and gave her a big hug and she hugged him back for the first time since she had been there. He then pulled her back and said, "I still love you Morgan even if you don't love me anymore." "Oh, Bradley, I do love you still but I don't see your father letting me into the family when I have nothing to bring in." Morgan said sadly. "If your haven't noticed but you are part of the family. My father just doesn't show it." "Then why is he paying me?" Morgan asked. "Simple, he wants you to have spending money." With a big smile he walked out the door.

The next morning Bradley called out of work. He wanted to spend the day with Morgan. He wanted to show her just how much he loved her. He wanted Morgan to love him back so much that she would say yes the next time he asked her.

They dropped the girls off at school and instead of going back to the house like they did every morning so Bradley could leave for work. Bradley headed for town with Morgan. Morgan just looked at him in shock. "Umm... Don't you have to be at work soon?" Morgan asked Bradley. "Not today" was all he said.

After a few minutes Bradley looked over at Morgan and said with a big smile on his face, "I wanted to spend the day with you. So, we could get to know each other better." Better he said? What is he wanting to do? He knew her better than anyone.

Being Friday Bradley took Morgan out for breakfast and then to see a show and then to lunch. They saw Step Up. It was a movie about young kids that were in a dance school and were in a dance contest. Bradley wanted to go slow with Morgan. He didn't want to rush anything and make her leave. He planned on asking her to marry him at the twins sixth birthday. This gave him nine months to get her to fall head over heels in love with him so that she would say yes this time. He already spoken to his father about this and he was on board. His father had promised not to get in the way of anything that Morgan wished to do. Even if that means she got a job while the girls were in school during the week. So the hard part was getting Morgan in the mood to say yes. Today was date number one with her and he hoped for many more with her.

Morgan really enjoyed her day out with Bradley. But in a way it was weird because they had always been out with James. Now that he was gone it was just her and Bradley going out and doing something. A little piece of her heart will always be with James. Morgan needed to remind herself and for that she had to move on for herself and the girls. Morgan was going to start now. James was her past, her teen years. Bradley is the now and maybe her forever. Only time will tell.

While Morgan and Bradley were out enjoying their free time without the two girls, Bradley asked Morgan if there was any place she wanted to go before he took her to dinner. Morgan thought for a few minutes and then said, "I would like to go see my parents." Bradley said, "I thought they passed away?" "They did, but I would like to go see their grave. I haven't been over there since I moved into your fathers home." Morgan said very sadly. "Okay, then we will go."

The grave yard was only a mile out of town. In fact it was the only grave yard their small town had. Morgan sat down next to the headstone and told her parents that she was doing good as was Rose and that she was even with little Mary now. She told them everything new she could think of. You guys would love Mary. She is just like Rose. The two girls get along great. It's like they have been together all along. Well, it's getting late. I love and miss you both so much. Morgan kissed her hand and placed it on the headstone. Then she got up and brushed off the dirt and told Bradley that she was ready to go.

As they were heading out of the grave yard Morgan and Bradley ran into Mrs. Heartman. She was down on the ground so they hadn't seen her. When Morgan looked down where Mrs. Heartman was at she seen, Beloved Son: James Edward Heartman. Morgan felt sick. Mrs. Heartman stood up and dusted off the dirt that was on her knees. "I see the unfaithful woman and the back stabbing friend are together again." Mrs. Heartman said cruelly. Bradley looked at Mrs. Heartman straight in the eyes and said that she needed to keep her mouth closed when she has nothing nice to say. Also, I would like you to be well mannered when you are around my daughters. Bradley took Morgan by her hand and left the grave yard and an open mouth Mrs. Heartman. Under Bradley's breath he said that he had always disliked that woman.

Bradley took Morgan to a small restaurant called Le Cafe. "This wasn't here when I lived here six years ago." Morgan said out loud. "Thought you would like to try something new. They are suppose to have great French food, but I've never tried them." Bradley smiled at Morgan, "Shall we be guinea pigs tonight?" Morgan smiled back and said, "Why not. It's not like it will kill us. Just don't make me eat snails," teased Morgan. Bradley took Morgan by the hand and together they went inside to eat. Bradley ordered for the two of them and twenty minutes later their food was in front of them. It was roasted duck and glazed baby carrots and mash potatoes with duck gravy. For drinks they had red wine. There was enough on their plates for two and a good thing too, for the price was a killer. Bradley even got dessert, chocolate cheese cake. Morgan looked up at Bradley and said that she was ready to go home. It was almost Mary and Rose's bedtime and she wanted to be the one to put them to bed.

CHAPTER 10

Morgan and Rose have been living with Mr. Baker, Bradley, and Mary now for seven months. Morgan couldn't believe that they have been there for so long. It was already December first.

The two girls came running in after school, "Mamma! Mamma! Guess what?!" The girls yelled. Morgan had the girls sit down in the kitchen while Mrs. Golden made them a snack of apple slices and peanut butter. The girls sat down and told Mrs. Golden thank you. With apples in their mouth they tried to tell their mamma the news of the day. This is how it came out, "Weave gurt to bez in a glade. Morgan smiled and told the girls to tell her without the apples in their mouth's. The girls took a big drink of their milk, then they tried again. The girls cleared their throat just like their grandfather. Then they spoke, "We get to be in a play, mamma." "Oh, that's great girls, we need to tell daddy and grandpa when they come home from work." Morgan told the girls.

That night at dinner the two girls told their daddy and grandpa about the play at school. Their grandpa, Mr. Baker asked the girls if they had a paper asking if the parent's needed to do or get anything? The girls didn't know. So, Morgan went and got their book bags. Inside their take home folder was a letter telling the parent's everything they needed to know about the school play. Morgan read the letter out loud. The letter said this:

Dear Parent's, This is a letter to inform you that your child is going to be in this years Christmas play. Any parent is allowed to come help with the set and with the costumes. After the play we will be having a little

Christmas party for the kids. Please send me a note weather you will be helping out and/or if you will be sending anything for the party. Thank You, Miss Nikki.

When Morgan was done reading the letter Mr. Baker said that he would make sure Miss Nikki had anything and everything for the play and the party. He would do anything to make this great for his two granddaughter's. Morgan said that she would help with the play setting and with the costumes. Bradley said that he would help the girls on knowing their lines and with the songs they were going to sing. This made the two girls very happy. Morgan filled out the form and made sure she wrote that she, Bradley and Mr. Baker would help with everything and that Mrs. Golden would make cookies for the party. According to the return sheet, the play and party is next week. We have a week to get the girls and the set ready.

Every night after dinner Bradley and the girls practiced their lines and the songs they would sing. The girls loved spending all this time with their daddy, especially Rose. This will be Rose's first Christmas with a daddy. Rose was glad that her and her mamma came here and stayed. This had been the best year that she could remember. She had a complete family like all the other kids in her class. Rose loved her family and hoped that they stay together forever. Not only was she happy but her mamma looked happy too. Mamma always had a smile. Best of all mamma didn't cry all the time like before they came here.

The night before the play Morgan had the girls try on their angel costumes. Morgan had made them herself. Mr. Baker wanted to have them special ordered but Morgan had told him that she wanted to make them herself. He had given in to what she wanted to do. Morgan had also made all of the kids costumes. Morgan was really good at sewing. The parents had thanked her and had told her that they were really good. That maybe she should open a little shop. Morgan had smiled and thanked them but she wasn't sure if she should do that, not with two small girls. Morgan wanted them to have all her free time, that a shop would make it hard for her to be with the two girls.

The night of the play Mr. Baker, Bradley and even Mrs. Golden came to watch the two girls. The play had Santa, his wife, the eight reindeer's, five elves, and six snow angels. They sang, Here Comes Santa, Jingle Bells and We Wish You A Merry Christmas And A Happy New Year. All the kids looked and did great. Mr. Baker had hired professionals to do the set so everything looked so life like. At the end of the play everyone clapped for the kids as they all took a bow. All the kids had fun doing the play. The kids told Mary and Rose that their family was the best.

After the play the kids and their families went to Miss Nikki's classroom for the party. Mrs. Golden had made sugar cookies in different shapes made just for Christmas. They were also filled with chocolate. The kids loved the cookies. They was also cupcakes, fruit punch and little stockings filled with candy, thanks to Mr. Baker. He even made sure that the kids that had older sister's and brother's or younger ones had stockings too. All the kids thanked Mr. Baker for the stockings.

On the ride home the girls were talking to their grandpa very softly so that their mamma and daddy couldn't hear. The girls were telling their grandpa that they wanted to do something special for their mamma and daddy for Christmas. Mr. Baker said that they could plan something over Christmas break. Mary was happy to have her mamma with her this year. She was really enjoying having a twin sister too. The whole ride home the two girls talked with just their grandpa. Every little bit one of the girls would look to see if mamma or daddy was listening.

When they got home the two girls wanted to stay up and keep talking to their grandpa but daddy said that they had to get to bed for school in the morning. Morgan told the girls to come on and she would brush their hair before they went to bed. The two girls ran up the stairs yelling, "Come on mamma," and they were giggling the whole way up to their bedroom. Morgan couldn't help but giggle with them. The girls always made her laugh and smile.

At the top of the stairs Morgan could hear the two girls saying that they beat mamma to their bedroom. So, Morgan walked up very quitely and went, "Boo!" to the two girls. Both the girls screamed and then started giggling really hard. At the same time the girls said, "You scare us mamma, that's not nice." Yet the girls had big smiles on their faces.

Morgan brushed their hair after they had their p.j.'s on. She was getting them tucked in when Bradley came in to see what what taking Morgan so long with the girls. Rose looked at her daddy and said, "Hugs and kisses daddy, that why mamma late." Mary go's, "Yeah, that right, we need lots of hugs and kisses from mamma and you daddy." Bradley smiled and gave each girl big hugs and sweet kisses on their foreheads. Then Morgan did the same.

As they were heading out the door Rose asked, "If daddy gave mamma any kisses before bed too?" Morgan blushed and said, "No, daddy doesn't give me any." Mary yells, "Daddy, you give mamma kisses too, right now!" Rose said, "Yeah!" To make the girls happy he had Morgan look at him and he kissed her on the forehead. The girls laughed and said, "No, daddy that not right. On her lips like the other daddy's did tonight." The two girls giggled. Morgan was blushing very red and Bradley asked her if it was alright with her, as it was to make the girls happy. Morgan nodded her head yes. Bradley gulped and cleared his throat. He then leaned in and gave Morgan her first kiss on the lips in over five years.

That was it they both lost it. No one else was in the room anymore. It was just them. Morgan brought her arms up and around Bradley's neck and pulled him closer. Bradley gladly came as close as he could get and deepened the kiss. Morgan let out a sigh and that was when they heard the giggling and clapping. Bradley and Morgan opened their eyes real fast and jumped back from each other. Morgan blushed and was saying, "Sorry." Bradley looked over to the girls who both stopped at his look and they laid back down. Bradley looked down sadly. "Okay girls you got what you wanted, now bedtime," he said breathlessly to the girls. "Night mamma and daddy. We wub you. Please, no be mad." They said with tears in their eyes. Morgan looked at both of them. "I will never be mad at you two girls, just myself for acting that way in front of you both." Mary looked at her mamma and said, "But that what mamma and daddy's do. I see them at school tonight." Morgan looked over at Bradley for a little help but he looked like he want to agree with Mary. Bradley said, "Mamma and daddy don't like to kiss in front of you girls, that's all," he said with a very big smile. Morgan still looking at him rolled her eyes. "Good night girls. We will see you in the morning. Mamma and daddy need to talk. Love you girls." Bradley said as he and Morgan left the room with two happy little girls in bed.

"What do we need to talk about?" Morgan asked not looking at Bradley. "Oh, I think you know." Bradley said with a smile. "Fine, but not in the hall." Morgan said. "Fine with me, my room, it's at the end of the hall away from everyone." Bradley said. "That's fine but I'm getting out of these jeans and getting my bed pants on first." Morgan said. As she walked into her room Bradley started to walk in too. "Just where do you think you are going?" Morgan asked with her eyebrow's raised. "Well... I...thought... I'll just wait out here." Bradley said shutting her door.

Inside Morgan giggled, aw just like in high school, she thought to herself. Wonder if he's still just as sexy looking and good in bed. Whoa... Man, I haven't thought about that in a long time. I'm sure he's been with other girls since me anyways. Even though he has been my only one. It would be nice to have his touch again, if only for a little bit. No! I would just want it more and it would drive me crazy. He will get tried of us being here or at least me. I doubt he still loves me. Of course that kiss was great! It took me back to my senior year in high school. That one great night. Then look where it left me. Ugh! That was my fault. I did this to my girls. Maybe I should just leave. Give Rose the life she should og had from the start. I don't know, I can't leave the girls not now. I love them both. I love being around Mary and watching the two girls play together. They need each other as much as I need them. Guess I better get this talk over with, with Bradley.

Morgan opened her door, "Okay let's go talk," she said to Bradley. Bradley just stared at her with wide open eyes. "What?" Morgan asked. Bradley cleared his throat. "I thought you were putting umm... bed pant's on?" "I did." Morgan said looking down and blushed. Well, that would teach her to talk to herself while getting dressed for bed. She had gotten into her "If I get lucky" clothes and put them on without thinking. So, with Bradley still staring she asked, "Do I need to change?" Right away Bradley says, "No! My umm... room is uhh... this way." He took her hand and walked her to his room. Morgan thought is was funny and cute because his hand was really sweaty.

When they got to Bradley's room Bradley excused himself into his bathroom to change. As Morgan looked around she saw that he also had a seating area by a window to read. There was a book on the table and a picture of Mary as a toddler. He had a rather small dresser with a mirror on it and Morgan could see her outfit very clearly. Oh my! No wonder he had sweaty hands and she giggled. She had put on her new black silky mini shorts and matching mini tank top. She sure didn't look like she had twin girls five years ago. Boy, she didn't notice she looked this good. No wonder all the guy's looked at her, but she don't care. She wants one man and she hopes he still wants her after all these years. She turned and looked at the bed and saw that next to it was three picture's of all four of them? She only knew of two picture's that were taken. One was when it was the last day they were together with the girls at a month old and one was from their first birthday. This one is of us at the hospital. Odd, I don't remember this one. She smiled at them. She reached out and was touching them when Bradley walked out of his bathroom. He looked to be freshly showered, shaved and wearing shorts. Bradley cleared his throat and said, "I see you found my favorite picture's of my family. "When did you have this picture taken of us at the hospital? Morgan asked. Bradley walked over to his bed and looked at his picture's. "It was taken right after they cleaned the girls up. You were kind of out of it. I had wanted to remember that day forever, so I had a nurse take the picture for me. It's my most prized picture that I have of my family. The one I always wanted after you told me you were expecting my baby."

Morgan was surprised and sadden because she didn't think she was worthy of Bradley's love back then. She didn't want to be rejected by Bradley's family, that's she didn't think how it would affect Bradley. Back then she was only thinking of her feelings when she should of thought of his as well. She was seeing how wrong she was back then. She was only eighteen when she had the girls. She was hating herself for the pain she caused Bradley and Mary. She wished she could go back to when Bradley first asked her to marry him. She would of said yes. Now, it's too late. She hurt him so bad by keeping Rose away all these years. She thought that by saying no to him that he would of found a nice rich girl to help him raise Mary. She was doing what she thought was best. If he still wanted to marry her she would say yes. She knows now that she would be accepted by Mr. Baker. Now all she needed to do was prove to Bradley that she is ready to be married to him forever.

It was the night before Christmas and the two girls were putting the final touches on the Christmas tree. Rose was so excited. She never had a tree before. So, helping daddy and grandpa put things onto the tree was fun. Rose was setting on the floor with Mary and mamma stinging popcorn on different colored stings so they could be put onto the tree. When the girls finished with the popcorn strings and hung them on the tree they ran to grandpa to finish with their surprise for mamma and daddy. Grandpa told the girls that everything was ready for the morning.

Morgan and Bradley then took the two girls up to bed. Morgan kissed the girls good night and gave them each a big hug. Bradley did the same. Morgan and Bradley told the girls to get to sleep really fast so Santa would come. "In the morning you two are to come get us up first. Then we can go down stairs after we get grandpa up, Bradley told them with a big smile. "O'tay daddy," they giggled. Morgan and Bradley left the room together. Bradley shut the door and when he turned around Morgan was just shutting her bedroom door.

The two girls were up bright and early Christmas morning. The two girls split up Mary ran and got Morgan up while Rose went and got Bradley up. Mary ran into Morgan's room and then she crawled up next to Morgan on the bed. She laid her head next to Morgan and she took her little arms and wrapped them around Morgan and said, "Mamma up now. Mamma we are up. Mamma!" Morgan jumps up and rolls onto the floor. "Ow, Mary, are you okay?" Morgan asked while rubbing her bottom. "You said to come get you up when we got up," Mary smiled down at Morgan. "Okay, I'm up where is Rose?" "Getting daddy up," Mary said bouncing on the bed. "Okay, let's go get daddy up" "Yay!" Mary yelled and grabbed Morgan's hand and pulled her out the bedroom towards daddy's room. Bradley was being awoken about the same way except Rose was jumping on the bed yelling, "Daddy up time. Daddy up time! Daddy, daddy, daddy, DADDY!" That one got him up. "Rose, what are you doing?" Bradley asked as he pulled the pillow over his face. "No, daddy, up, you say so!" Rose yelled. Bout that time Morgan and Mary came in the room. Mary ran over and jumped on the bed too. Now Bradley had two little jumping beans on his bed. Bradley sighed, "Okay, okay, daddy is getting up." Morgan giggled at the sight in front of her. "Oh, you think this is funny, mommy?" Bradley teased as he grabbed Morgan's hand and pulled her onto him. Morgan just kept giggling and the two girls were giggling too.

As they were all laughing Mr. Baker walks to the door and clears his throat, "Why is everyone still in bed? It looks like Santa was here last night." The two girls turned and jumped off the bed and ran to Mr.

Baker yelling, "Santa, Santa. Come on mamma and daddy. Grandpa said Santa was here, yay." With that the two girls ran out the room. Mr. Baker stood there laughing. "You two better get down there before those two little angels turn into little devils and open all those gifts without this," Mr. Baker held up his camera with a smile. Bradley got up off his bed and helped Morgan stand. "Let's go stop our girls before we end up with no pictures of their first Christmas together." Bradley said still holding Morgan's hand in his.

As Morgan, Bradley and Mr. Baker walked down the stairs they could hear the two girls giggling and shaking gifts. "Okay, girls you both need to wait for us to get down there with grandpa's camera." Bradley yelled from the stairs. "O'tay daddy," both the girls yelled and giggled some more. Mr. Baker rounded the corner first. He winked at the girls as Bradley and Morgan rounded the corner last. "Okay since this is Rose's and mommy's first Christmas with us I think they should get the first gifts. What do you think Mary?" "I say mamma and daddy go first." "I say so too," Rose said. "Looks like it's settled then." Mr. Baker said with a smiled. "Okay? Why are we going first? This day is for you two girls not us." Bradley said to the girls. "No tis time daddy and mamma go first," the girls said together. "Okay. We will go first." Bradley said with his hands up. The two girls giggled at daddy. "Let's see, I believe this one is for mommy?" "No, daddy we give you what to open." Both the girls said. The two girls went behind the tree and together they brought a box out and said, "This is for both of you. Mamma, daddy you open same time. Grandpa, you take pickture of them." Mary said. "Okay girls grandpa is ready." Morgan and Bradley had the box between them and the each started tearing a side open. When it was unwrapped their gift from the two girls was a new video camcorder. "Bradley and Morgan said, "Thank you girls." Then gave them a hug each. Mr. Baker says, "It's already charged and ready to use."

After that they girls got handed gifts after gifts to open. Bradley video taped and Mr. Baker snapped shots after they showed what the unwrapped. Rose got a new bike, roller skates, lots of clothes, six new shoes, lots of stuffed toys and baby dolls. Mary got the same things. There was one gift left and it was from Morgan to the girls. It was a big box too. Both the girls did just like mamma and daddy did for their combined gift. They ripped the paper off and under the paper was a big old fashion doll house.

It came with all the furniture and some dolls just for it. The girls looked over at Morgan and without warning they both jumped on her knocking her flat on her bottom. "Thank you mamma. We love it! "They were two very happy little girls. Bradley and Mr. Baker looked at her and mouthed, "How?" Morgan just smiled and said, "Saved since I have been here." She was glad the girls like their gift. Bradley had a small box for Morgan to open. She took the box and opened it. Inside was a mother's ring with her birthstone of February and the girls being June. It also had their names and birth date which was June first. Morgan looked at the ring and with tears in her eyes said, "Thank you." Morgan placed it on her right hand and the ring fit perfectly. Morgan had also gotten some reading books and a beautiful necklace and earring set form Mr. Baker. Bradley got a new watch from Morgan and some cute neck ties from the girls. Mr. Baker got new golf clubs from the two girls and a new watch from Morgan. They even had a necklace for Mrs. Golden.

The girls went around and gave everyone hugs and said that they had the best Christmas ever. That the best part was that they had their daddy and mamma this year.

CHAPTER 11

Morgan couldn't believe her and Rose have been with Mary for a whole year. It felt like they just got there. Rose and Mary were two peas in a pod. They did everything together. I do mean everything. Back in March both the girls got chicken pox's. The girls were so itchy. They walked around looking like they roll around in strawberry yogurt. Every night for three weeks the girls got an oatmeal bath to help with the itch. They were happy when they were all better. Morgan had never been so tired since the girls were a few weeks old. They manage to get through kindergarten with good marks. Mr. Baker was so proud of the girls that he took them for ice cream every night after dinner for a week. The girls loved that.

Now it was their sixth birthday. Morgan was in the kitchen with Mrs. Golden helping her make chocolate chip cakes for the girls. This year the girls were going to have their birthday at the zoo. The girls wanted all the kids in their class to come so we had a lot of planning to do the last month. The zoo said that they had a special place where the kids could have their party. The party is to start at two and it was only eight in the morning. They needed four cakes and they had to load the van up with everything we were taking there with us. Which was a lot. We have to take the van which Bradley was going to drive with Mr. Baker riding with him, Then I was taking the car with the girls and Mrs. Golden. Bradley was busy packing the van with the gifts for the girls, the balloons and air tanks, gift bags for all the kids, and we were going to have hot dogs. So, Bradley still needed to go to the store and get ice, hot dogs, hot dog buns, mustard, ketchup, chips, and kool-aid juices.

While Bradley, Morgan, and Mrs. Golden were baking and packing,

Mr. Baker had the girls at the city park playing and being out of the way. He offered and we said to go ahead. Although, they missed hearing the girls running around and laughing about something. The house was actually too quite for once. But they manage to get everything done by noon. Now, they were waiting for the girls to come in so they could take a bath and get dressed.

The girls came running in yelling, "Look what grandpa got us each!" They exclaimed. They each held up a new necklace. Rose had a purple butterfly with blue stones for eyes and Mary had a pink butterfly with blue stone eyes. Morgan looked at their necklaces and told the girls that they were very pretty just like them. "Now, let's go get changed for the party and no dresses." "Aw," was the girls reply.

The girls were bathed, dressed and really to leave for the zoo party. Morgan had put the girls in jean capri's paired with baby doll tops. Rose had a blue top and Mary had a green top on. She then put the girls in pigtails with bands that matched their tops. Their hair looked so cute with their natural curls. The girls ran to their daddy and asked, "Do we look pretty, daddy?" Bradley looked at his girls and said, "You girls are as beautiful as your mamma." The girls ran around saying, "Yay, we look like mamma. We are boo-tee-full."

They finally got the girls loaded and Mrs. Golden into the car. Bradley and Mr. Baker were in the van with all the stuff that was needed for the party. Morgan was following Bradley on the highway and the girls were singing songs that they had learned in school. Morgan kept looking in the rear view mirror at the two girls and smiling. The girls always made her smile. Even Mrs. Golden was smiling and trying to sing along with the girls. It was a funny site.

Half an hour later they were pulling into the zoo's parking spot in front of their main office so they could check in and get help packing everything to the party spot. Bradley and grandpa went into the office to let them know they were there. Morgan had Mrs. Golden take the girls in to the aquarium house to see the fish and other water life animals while they went and set things up for the party. They had forty-five minutes to get everything set up before the party was to start. Thank goodness they were getting help from the staff at the zoo.

As they were taken to the party spot the zoo had a surprise waiting for them. Hanging in two different spots were pinata shaped like monkey's. Each monkey had the girls names on it. Morgan and Bradley were taken back, they had not expected anything from the zoo. This will surly make the two girls happy. Bradley and Morgan thanked the staff for the help and the surprise.

With ten minutes to spare Mr. Baker went to go get the girls and Mrs. Golden for the party. The girls were ready for their party to start. When the girls seen Mr. Baker they asked if ant of their friends were here yet? Grandpa looked down and said, "No one was there when I left to come get my little princesses and you Mrs. Golden." "Hurry grandpa, we need to get there before everybody else. Come on Mrs. Golden," the girls tugged on their hands.

When the girls, Mr. Baker and Mrs. Golden got to the party site the first few guest were getting there too. The girls ran over to see their friends Alice and Connor Price. They were the other set of twins in their class. Their birthday was last month. They had just turned six too. The four kids were setting at one of the benches talking about all the animals they wanted to pet at the petting zoo after they had hot dogs and cake. Alice and Rose wanted to pet the goats and feed them first and Conner and Mary wanted to pet the baby ducks first. As they were taking Brooke Owen and Heath Walker showed up. Then Skye Roberts, Dimitri Leeks, Faith Rowens, Ty Burk, Ryan Black, Emma Lee, Marco Scotts and their teacher Miss Nikki showed up along with all their cousins, aunts, and uncles. The party was ready to start.

To start the party off was the visit to the petting zoo. All the kids went in the pen with Miss. Isis one of the zoo workers that were helping with the party. Morgan had Bradley use the cam recorder they got for Christmas from the girls. Every now and then Morgan would call the kids attention so they could get faces on video. Most of the time they were getting the back of their heads. The kids were all laughing and having fun while all the different baby animals came up to them and either sneezed on them of was licking at they legs, arms, and some even got their faces licked. Morgan and Bradley were glad the kids were having a great time.

After an hour in the petting zoo the kids came out and all got their hands and faces washed at the little sink they had outside the petting zoo pens. The kids were still laughing and even tried to get their parents wet with the water when they weren't trying to get each other wet. "Okay, everyone, we are going to go back over to the party site and we are going to let the kids hit the pinata's," Miss Isis announced. All the kids yelled, "YAY!!" They walked back over to the party spot and the birthday girls got to go first with their own pinata.

All the kids took turns hitting them. They were going on their fourth round when Dimitri broke Rose's open and Skye broke Mary's open. Inside were dum dum pop's, stickers, fake animal tattoo's and rubber animals. Morgan gathered all the items up and split everything with the younger kids. Morgan was glad that it split even with all the younger kids. The kids were very happy with their pinata goodies.

It was time for the gifts. The two girls ended up with a lot of new toys. They even got some coloring books and reading books to help them start first grade. The last few things they opened was from grandpa he got them each angel baby dolls, Mrs. Golden got them each new hair bows and other hair things. Last was their gifts from mamma and daddy. Daddy got them a play kitchen and a play grocery store. Mamma got them toy pots, pans, and other dishes along with a play shopping cart with lots of different foods. The girls tanked everyone for their gifts.

After all the gifts were open Miss Isis took everyone around to see all the different animal and explained what each animal was and how they were different. When they got to the reptile house none of the little girls wanted to go inside but all the boys did. So, while Miss Isis took the boys inside another zoo helper came over to take the girls to the butterfly house. They were to meet up with the boys at the polar bear pen.

While the kids were off seeing all the different animals Morgan, Bradley, Mrs. Golden, Mr. Baker and the other adults started to pack up everything and to clean up after the party. The party was coming to an end. Morgan looked around and was amazed how her's and Rose's life had changed in a year. They were with Mary and Rose had her daddy at last. Morgan was smiling to herself when Mrs. Golden came over to her to ask if she wanted her to start taking the stuff back to the van. Morgan said, "Yes, I'll have Bradley and Mr. Baker go get a few of the zoo helpers to help load up."

While Morgan was talking with Mrs. Golden, Bradley was talking to his family about one more surprise that he had in stored for today. He told them that after all the girls friends and their parents left he was going to do something and only wanted the family here for it. Well, this made the family wonder what he had in stored. The girls got all their gifts from what they could see by looking around. Not one gift was still wrapped. Bradley seen that they were taking about the surprise and were starting to get a little loud about it. He turned to them and asked for them to be quite about the surprise. So, they complied and did speak about again. They just watched him to see if would give a hint of the surprise.

After two hours of walking around the zoo all the kids were ready to go home. Even the two girls were getting tired. They said their good bye's to their friends and sat down on the benches. It was now six at night and the girls were tired and starting to get hungry. The girls called their daddy over to them. Bradley walked over there and bent down to see what they needed. "We are getting hungry, daddy. Is it time to leave yet?" They asked daddy. "No, not yet. Give me a few more minutes then we can leave." He smiled at the girls and gave them each a kiss on the forehead.

Mr. Baker and Mrs. Golden came back and told Bradley and Morgan that the van was packed and ready when they were. Bradley smiled, "Good. Okay. Can I please have everyone come sit down close together? Morgan sit here and girls I would like to have each of you on either side of mamma. Dad, you have the cam recorder ready?" "Sure do son, ready when you are." Mr. Baker said with a big smile on his face. "Okay, everyone please be quite for a few minutes." Bradley cleared his throat and looked at Morgan and the girls. "Morgan." Bradley began and bent on one knee. Everyone gasped including Morgan. "Morgan, will you do me the honor and become my wife so, we made make our family one hundred percent whole?" Everyone stared at Morgan and waited for her reply.